About the Auth

Michael Robinson had a difficult childhood schizoaffective disorder at the age of 17.

At the age of 20, Robinson joined the 4th Brittalian Parachute Regiment, and later the 3rd Britallian Prince of Wales Own Regiment. Upon passing out, he was awarded "Most Improved Recruit."

Later into his military career, Robinson volunteered for the arduous "Cambrian Patrol" A type of special forces training with a view of joining the SAS. However, during deployment, in the Brecon Beacons, Robinson succumbed to Hypothermia, and was ultimately sacked from the Army on Christmas Eve after they looked into his medical records.

From here, Robinson ended up in HM Prison Hull and was later locked up indefinitely under Section 37/41.

He remained locked up for about 3 years and on release wrote about his experiences in his Autobiography 'Sectioned: The Book The NHS Tried To Ban' on Amazon Kindle.

As well as Soldier, other jobs Robinson has done include Drummer for two successful groups, Carer at a special needs school, Chef, Bouncer, Driver and Minder for a Hull Escort Agency.

Also, he has an NVQ in Catering, Diploma in Uniformed Public Services and has read Law with Criminology at University.

Robinson has been married to Julie, his long-term partner for 10 years and he continues to support mental health campaigns with help from his local MP and other Government agencies.

This includes working with The Heads Together campaign, MIND and other mental health charities.

(You Tube: "Head Together Campaign, Michael 'Robbo' "Robinson.")

He regularly helps the homeless in Hull and other persons/groups in need where he can.

Other books Robinson has written include 'Sectioned: The Book The NHS Tried To Ban', (Autobiography.)

The Killing Moon (Fiction)

Dirty Laundry – Confessions Of An Escort Agency Minder (Autobiography)

He is currently working on Eliminator (Fiction.) To be released soon.

All of Robinson's works are available at https://michaelsrobinsonauthor.com

Also available at Amazon Kindle.

Thief Taker

Chapter One

It was hard to believe that Catherine Harrison once had it all, from the women's hostel which was now her home. As she sat on her single bed on her damp, ground floor room on the Boulevard, things were now a world away from what they had been. Even she had to admit that her problems stemmed from her addiction. Catherine never liked to admit to anything, least of all to herself.

She looked at the makeshift tin foil crack pipe on the floor to see if there were any white rocks left in it, but she knew that there was none. She had done it all in once she got home. When did she get home? She couldn't remember. Sleep was something to have between hits, sometimes day, sometimes night. It wasn't like she had a normal sleep pattern like the rest of the world had. A job may have made a difference, but Catherine's job was taking crack. Get up, get high, maybe eat, get high, maybe sleep. It was one long monotonous roundabout.

Around her room were her clothes. Shoes and makeup in no particular order and arranged by chaos along the floor. Also, amongst the mess, were her books. When she was straight, she loved to read. She hadn't been able to read since her addiction got crazy as she couldn't concentrate on anything for more than five minutes if it didn't involve getting high.

She thought back to her past. She wasn't a footballer's wife, or some sort of socialite. She was a madame for an exclusive escort agency. The agency was based in Hull in the North of England. It was the only agency in the area and therefore, she had the monopoly. Clients would ring from places as far away as York, Lincoln and Scarborough. At its height, the agency had at least 20 girls on the books. Some of the escorts looked like models while others were students and some were single mothers, but all were willing to trade sex for money.

The penthouse suite from which Catherine ran her business was on Victoria Dock. An old timber dock that had been transformed into fashionable apartments. Everything was paid up front in cash. Catherine had the best designer shoes and clothes. Sky tv, tickets to any concert or event that she wanted, plus at least two drivers on standby at any given time to take her anywhere she needed or desired to go to. The main thing was her two kids. One girl aged 13, and one boy aged 9. The money she earnt from the agency paid for them both to have the best lifestyle that she could afford, this included holidays frequently and attending private schools.

Some of the agency's clients included local celebrities and sports figures. High ranking police officers were on the books, plus at least one judge. Most of the client base, however, was made up of your everyday John's. Lonely men on Friday nights who had been unable to pull whilst out, or couples who wanted to fulfil their husbands' fantasies or bisexual women who wanted the best of both. Then there were the pervs. Clients that had a particular kink. This was fine, you could charge extra for these kinks. However, the rule was no kids and no animals, other than that anything went.

Catherine had made a lot of money over the years. Far too much money. First it was the coke every couple of months at a party or on a night out with the girls - the coke took over after a while and it wasn't the same as the first time. In came the heroin and soon after the crack. The crack took the apartment first. One by one, the girls left, like rats leaving a sinking ship. The drivers soon followed, disheartened by Catherine's lifestyle. Soon there was no calls coming in as all the decent girls had left meaning that she no longer had money coming in, and what cash there was, went straight to her dealer.

Then the fatal blow. The crack took the kids. The courts granting custody to her ex, once it became apparent of Catherine's chaotic lifestyle.

All that was left was the book of contacts from the agency, her suitcase and now a dingy room at the women's hostel.

Catherine didn't dwell for too long, she had other things to deal with. The phone rang. She picked it up and looked at the screen. It was yet another dealer that she owed money to after a layout. Instead of answering it, Catherine made for the door, walked down the corridor and into the world.

It was time to get high.

Chapter Two

Jake Sylvester was head of child adoption and child safeguarding at East Riding Council. He was also a predatory paedophile. If being a gay man in the 80's was taboo, then it wasn't now. There were even laws to encourage and protect his status. It was politically correct to encourage the gay community to apply for roles within the council and were actively encouraged to seek advancement in these roles by positive discrimination. To Jake Sylvester, this meant that he was able to actively manipulate and have access to young children at any given notice, under the cloak of being accepted by society as the new normal, he abused hundreds of children well under the radar. No one ever questioned his integrity. As a young gay man, he used his sexuality to climb the greasy pole to become head of child services.

Outside his office in the town of Beverley, East Yorkshire, were Mr. and Mrs. Smith. Both were apprehensive about their meeting with the head of child services.

"Come in, please sit down" said Jake as he answered the door to his large Victorian office. Both obliged but Mrs. Smith was the first to speak whilst holding her handbag with both hands on her lap "Mr. Sylvester, thank you for seeing us both. It's been six months since we've both seen our boys, Matthew and Peter." Mrs. Smith continued "but things have settled down now at home, Mr. Smith hasn't had a drink in five months straight and we have managed to get the rent and council tax arrears down after my husband lost his job on the dock, also I've managed to get a part time cleaning job" Jake held up his hand to pause Mrs. Smith, but she continued. "We were wondering if it was time for the boys to come home now?"

"Mrs Smith," Jake replied "I realise that this is a difficult time, but I have to think of the welfare of both Matthew and Peter. You must remember how there was next to no food in your house, also how Mr Smith was with us when we were only trying to help the boys. I am afraid that the council has decided to put both Matthew and Peter into long-term care."

Mr Smith, who had remained silent throughout spoke for the first time, "We were told that it wasn't permanent - that it would be a few weeks."

"Mr Smith" Jake replied "what you have to understand is that we want mummies and daddies to have a stable home to raise the children in."

Mr Smith interrupted "You let gays adopt, don't you?"

Jake was defensive and it showed "What do you mean?"

Mr Smith continued, "well, if it's two men adopting, who's the Mummy and who's the Daddy?"

"Mr Smith, with this type of behaviour we cannot let the children be party to."

Mrs Smith took his arm and said "John, leave it" and he immediately regained his composure.

Jake stood up and held out his arm as an abrupt end to the meeting "I am afraid we'll have to leave it there for now" as he took both Mr and Mrs Smith out of his office. With dignity, Mrs Smith took a hankie out of her purse just as Jake shut the door.

Outside the dejected couple stood, Mrs Smith spoke, "Well, we'll just have to wait a little while longer John." He looked at his wife with the same loss.

"I'm going for a walk; I'll see you back home." Mrs Smith knew that her husband was going to the pub and that he would be falling back into the drink. As he walked away, she called "John no!" But he was gone.

Back in the office, Jake Sylvester looked at his laptop. On the screen was images of John Smith - the younger boy being abused by Jakes husband. Jake smiled and closed the file.

Chapter Three

Catherine made her way from The Boulevard towards The Avenues. Maybe she could score at Sophie's. Sophie had been on the books as one of Cathy's escorts, and like Cathy, Sophie was addicted to crack cocaine. Sophie was pregnant and due any day. She was planning a home birth as she knew that the minute she gave birth in hospital, the child would be taken away by social services.

Sophie's partner and fellow junkie was Terry. Cath had never cared much for him. Not because he was a junkie, that was irrelevant and Cathy didn't discriminate, but because while Sophie worked for the agency, Terry would leach, get high, and live off Sophie's earnings. He had a nasty streak too as he could get violent when coming down. Terry tended to pick on the weak, usually to fund his habit. He had been known to burgle pensioners and even stealing and selling war medals that were never recovered. He had also served time for mugging a guy in a wheelchair. Whenever Cath would meet Sophie, Sophie's eyes and face were always bruised despite her attempt to cover them with cheap foundation. Lately, Sophie's face was bruised more and more. Terry would never do that to a man or anyone that could fight back.

Cathy reached Sophie's house on The Avenues. While most people were out at work, or had at least opened the curtains, Sophie's house always had the curtains drawn to keep out the light and to avoid any people walking by seeing what this home was – a crack house. The white paint on the front door showed signs of peeling and neglect, from a landlord who never cared who he rented it to as long as his money came in once a month. Cathy stepped inside and the smell of heat, bodies, drugs and sweat was a contrast to the fresh air outside. A TV blasted from the living room on the left while the thread bare carpet in the hall just about covered the floor leading to the stairs.

Cathy walked into the living room and Terry, along with another guy (who she didn't recognise) were both mooched out on the sofa. The heat from the electric fire cooking the living room. Terry was the first to speak "Alright Cath, after a smoke?"

"Yeah, can do, where's Sophie?" she asked.

"Upstairs with the baby" he replied.

"What, she's had it?" She asked puzzlingly.

"Yeah, came last night. Go and have a look".

Cathy climbed the stairs, anxious to see the newborn. Upon entering the bedroom, Sophie was sat on the bed cradling the new baby boy. "Hi Cath, come and have a look" smiled Sophie. Cath noticed that she had a new blackened eye but said nothing.

For the next half hour, the two girls talked about motherhood – with a tinge of pain whenever Cath spoke of her own children, but she took great comfort in holding the little man in her arms as if she almost had a connection with him.

Sophie then looked at Cath, there was something in her eyes that told Cath that whatever she was about to say was important. "Listen Cath" Sophie almost whispered, "I think Terry is up to something with the baby."

"What like?" Cathy asked quizzingly.

"I'm not sure but he said that he wants to take him out later and he won't tell me where."

Chapter Four

Catherine wouldn't have believed it, if it wasn't for the fact that she heard it. After an hour of smoking crack, she came round in the living room. She was alone but could hear Terry on the phone next door. At first, she thought it was just another deal being arranged, to just another punter. It was at that point that the penny dropped as he mentioned the baby.

"Yeah, two hours" said Terry "do whatever you want to him. Yeah four hundred quid, I will meet you tonight at Tesco on Hall Road."

Still stoned from the crack, Cath thought about it – what could she do? Who could she ring? Facing the facts, she had no one. All the decent friends in her life had left her a long time ago, when her addiction took over. It wasn't that they didn't care, they did, but Cath wouldn't listen. The police? No chance Cath thought, better odds on taking the baby then being a grass – she paused and thought again. Take the baby? She could take him to safety – away from Terry.

Terry entered the room. Sat down and lit the crack pipe again. Cath pretended to be asleep and out of it. Three long drags on his pipe, and he was slumped back into his chair, his eyes shut like he'd escaped into some beautiful dream. Catherine saw her chance. He'd be out for at least half an hour.

Cath made her way upstairs to Sophie and the baby. Entering the room, Sophie was also stoned with Terry's gear.

Catherine gently whispered, "Sophie wake up." It was in vain, Sophie was well out of it but she continued "Sophie come on, we have to get out of here"

Sophie groaned "What is it?"

"Terry is trying to rent the baby to a paedo, we have to get out of here."

"No Cath" replied Sophie, half in comatose.

"No Sophie, we have to go."

Sophie then mumbled, "Cath, just take him."

"No, we have to go together" she responded.

"Cath, just take the baby away from Terry."

Cath looked at Sophie for a second, her maternal instincts took over. Within a minute, she'd picked up the small child and wrapped him in a towel. She headed down the stairs right as the infant started to cry. She looked towards the living room door for any signs of movement from Terry, but there was not any. Her heart was beating so hard that she could feel it drumming in her chest. She had mere seconds to move. She headed out the door, closing it gently behind her. Once in the street, she hurried – to where, she did not know.

Chapter Five

Jake Sylvester called his husband during his lunch break. Arthur answered the phone within the first few rings.

"Hiya Lover, just ringing you to let you know that I'll be home early tonight so we could go out to ASK for something to eat if you want?"

Arthur responded, "I've already made plans for us tonight, we've got ourselves a plaything for a few hours."

Jake looked around cautiously to see if anyone was around "Ooo, you're a bad bitch, you know it's not my birthday! Who's this one anyway?"

Arthur replied, "A baby boy, he's a few hours old from The Avenues. I used to get coke from his dad and that's what put me onto him, but we've only got him for a few hours ducky."

"Oh well in that case, I'll make sure I'm home on time then."

"Don't make promises you can't keep lover." Arthur said teasingly.

"Ooo stop it you fake flirt."

"Okay, well I'll see you later, I love you."

"Love you more, bye."

Chapter Six

DCI Patrick Fisher was just about to leave the office when he got the call. A newborn baby had been taken, but the details were sketchy at best. Patrick had been on the police force for over twenty years now. He was a committed and dedicated Police Officer, but this had come at a price, three marriages and four children that he rarely saw – his current wife put up with the late nights, but it still put a strain on the marriage. Patrick was in his mid-fifties and nearing retirement, or as Pat thought, being put out to pasture and be forgotten.

Things had changed so much in the force since he had become a beat copper in the late 70's. Walking the mean streets of Hessle Road in Hull, for six years certainly toughened him up in the early days. As he was young and ambitious, promotions to CID soon followed. Patrick had worked on some high-profile murders in the city, some making national news. He had put away some very bad men, some with very high tariffs.

Things changed in the nineties though. First, there were the fresh new breed of talented coppers climbing up through the ranks. They were all like him when they first started, although Patrick would never admit it. They were dedicated, ambitious, but mainly arrogant. Even in his late twenties, Patrick felt old.

Then there were the rules. Criminals could get away with a lot more these days and coppers a lot less. In the nineties, CCTV picked up an image of a black guy chocking to death in cuffs in Queens Gardens police station. The images went viral as it came to light – and of course the family wanted money under the guise of "justice". The local press surged ahead with a campaign against Humberside Police. This meant officers were sacked, with some even receiving charges against them. The real travesty about the whole sorry episode was the fact the family had another brother in a medium secure hospital, and upon investigation, this poor bugger hadn't had a visit in years, he was basically left to rot inside the institution, by a family who couldn't care less. The force couldn't tell the press this for fear of bias against the family. Patrick hated the fact the family played the race card every chance they could.

This was the politics of the job now, with the good old days never returning. Patrick had a job to do now, so he grabbed his car keys and his suit jacket that had been hung over the back of the swivel chair and made his way to The Avenues. He just about remembered to text his wife that he was going to be home late again.

After leaving the crack house with Sophie's baby, Cath headed straight to her room at the hostel. She stopped at the corner shop on the way and paid with what money she had left for some items, shop lifting the rest including nappies and baby food. Cath was still stoned from the crack as she entered her room with the little man, she wished she were more organised. Carefully putting the infant on the bed, she cleaned him up and changed him – soon he would be hungry.

Catherine thought for a moment, she took out her mobile phone and rang Steve, she wondered if he would take her calls. After 4 rings, he picked up "Steve are you still in Leeds?"

"Yeah why, what's the matter?"

"Can you pick me up from the station when I ring you please?"

Steve replied, "Why have you got me the money you owe me for god knows how many jobs I've done for you?"

"Steve listen, I'm in trouble" she pleaded.

"No shit Sherlock" he responded, "when you started using that shit it was nothing but trouble, what you done, ripped off the wrong dealer?"

"No, it's nothing like that. Can you pick me up from Leeds station or not?" she added "please, just for old times sake."

"Well, I've got nowt else on now that I'm out of work. You'd better ring me when you get there."

"Okay, give me a few hours" she replied before hanging up.

Looking around the room one last time, Catherine grabbed what she could, including the baby before heading for Hull train station.

Chapter Seven

When Patrick arrived at the house on The Avenues, uniform was stood on the doorstep. Immediately they made a hole so Patrick could go inside and within seconds Patrick realised he was standing within a drug den. This meant there were going to be implications for the family of the missing child, also, before he spoke to anyone he asked himself if this was a kidnapping after a bad deal. Walking in the living room, both Sophie and Terry looked pathetic individuals sat together on the mucky, torn leather couch. Patrick introduced himself to the couple, and it was Terry who responded first, trying to keep his cards close to his chest "I don't know what happened officer" Terry said unconvincingly "I was asleep on the sofa when Sophie woke me and told me that the baby had gone."

"How many people were in the house at the time the baby went missing?" Patrick enquired. Again, it was Terry who spoke.

"Just my mate Al, but he wouldn't have taken her and then Cath turned up,"

"Okay, where's Al now?" Patrick asked.

"I don't know, I fell asleep like I said, so he probably went to work or something."

"Do you have a telephone number for Al?" the inspector questioned.

"Yeah, I might have one somewhere, but he doesn't normally keep it on."

"Okay, and who is this Cath?"

"Catherine Harrison" responded Terry. On hearing Cath's name, Patrick's ears popped up. Catherine Harrison was well known to the police as the local Madam. In fact, Patrick had interviewed her on more than a few occasions, but something didn't make sense. Sure, Cath was known to the police, but she was intelligent, savvy and a career Madam, but if Cath had been the one to take the baby, then Patrick suspected there must be a reason for it. Patrick made some more notes but was sure to give nothing away whilst interviewing the couple. He was adamant that he wanted them both in custody tonight, but first he would need some evidence. After finishing his notes, he stood up and politely asked if he could look around. Terry shifted in his seat uncomfortably but nodded yes.

Patrick left the room and meticulously made his way around the house. It was sparsely furnished and unclean. In the kitchen there were pans half filled with food and hardly used. The sink was just as disgusting, half filled with mucky plates and half filled with stagnant water that had likely been sat for days. The seasoned copper made his way upstairs, walking into Sophie and Terrys bedroom he saw where Sophie had given birth as dried blood and plasma was everywhere and he noted that on the side table was all kinds of drug paraphernalia. Quietly he undid the drawers and found exactly what he was looking for, under a book in the drawer, Patrick found three small see-through packets of what he could only assume was crack cocaine. He made his way downstairs, then collared one of the officers in uniform off the doorstep. "You, come with me. You, get me police van and forensics down here now. I want these two in custody as soon as possible." He returned to the living room with the young officer and placed both suspects under arrest for possession of a Class A substance. Terry began to protest as the officer put cuffs on him, but Sophie was beaten so she said nothing as she stared into the distance. Within twenty minutes a police van had arrived and was ready to take both suspects away. However, Sophie was taken first to Hull Royal Infirmary for assessment. This was going to be one of those cases Patrick thought to himself.

Chapter Eight

It was easy to get to Leeds from Hull station. The train company had a policy of giving a free ticket to any woman who at the ticket office said she was in danger and needed to leave the city and so the fact Cath had a newborn baby with her made her case all the more compelling to the lady working the ticket booth.

She rang Steve once on the train and as promised he met Catherine in the pickup bay of Leeds station in his Suzuki car. Steve had an affection for Cath despite the fact she'd screwed him over. He had worked for her for a good two years and became quite close over that time. He knew it was her dependency on the drugs that had made everything go so wrong. However, when Cath entered the passenger seat of his car, he was shocked to see her cradling a newborn baby.

"Fuck me Cath, when did you have a kid?"

"It's not mine," she replied "let's just get out of here and I'll fill you in."

Steve put the car in first and began to drive away. "Fuck me, Cath, if you've nicked a kid that must mean there's some serious shit going on."

"I had no choice. I've gotta protect him."

"Well we'd best get back to mine then, I've got a flat just outside the city center."

Back at Steve's flat, Steve made some coffee whilst Cath saw to the baby. She had managed to give him a full bottle and he started to settle. Steve placed both coffees on the round table in the living room and sat opposite them before he said "Okay, come on Cath, talk to me, what's going on?"

Cath took a deep breath and said "Steve, I wanna get clean."

"You've had years to get clean, why now?" was Steve's curt reply.

"I know I sound like any other junkie, but I really mean it and I want you to help me."

Steve took a deep breath and sighed. "The only way you're gonna get clean is if you go cold turkey."

"Yes, I know and ordinarily, I'd go to rehab, but I can't with this little one."

Steve had more questions. All the time, he watched her body language to judge whether she was bullshitting him or not. "What the fuck is the story with the baby then Cath?" He noticed how she cradled the infant as if it was her own, it was a maternal side to Cath that he hadn't seen before. This made her case all the more compelling.

Cath went on to explain how she'd gone to Sophie and Terry's to get high, and how she had overheard Terry pimping out the infant as if he was a piece of meat. Steve remembered both Sophie and Terry from the days when he worked for Cath and even though he hated working with the junkies, Sophie had been one of the easier ones to deal with. It soon became apparent that Cath was in a catch twenty-two position, had she gone to the police, she would've been ostracized. Looking at Cath's options, he saw she had very few of them. The one thing he was certain of though was the fact that Catherine was in trouble, and she was being genuine about it. Soon a world of shit would be coming her way. Steve figured that the police would already be out looking for Cath as well as the bounty on the baby's head. Steve had no doubt all the junkies would be talking about what she had done, which ultimately was a good thing since the way the drug community worked meant there would be a lot of rumours and dead ends for the police to follow. Steve knew the police would soon come knocking at his door if not tonight then in the next few days. Steve had heard enough. "Okay, I've got a mate in the regiment whose got a cottage in North Yorkshire. I'll have a word with him and see if you can stay there while you get clean. But the thing is Cath, you've gotta get clean if you wanna help that baby."

Cath took on board everything Steve had said, but even she was struggling as she began to come down and even now, she could just do with another hit but a cottage in the middle of nowhere was ideal. It meant she could get clean and not be tempted by the devil himself. Steve finished his coffee and said, "I'll ring him now, everything should be fine and then we'll get off in the next half an hour."

Leaving the room, Steve made the call to his oppo and just as expected, everything was fine. He would have to swing by Newcastle to pick up the key but other than that it would be a four-hour drive away. Steve re-entered the living room and found Cath asleep, he gently got onto his knees and held her hand before quietly whispering "Come on Cath, we're going. Everything's in place, we just need to get up there. On the way there, we'll swing by Argos and get a baby seat."

Within half an hour, Steve was on the A1. Cath realised that she'd had no right to ask Steve for anything as she knew full well that she had burned him on more than one occasion and ultimately, he was a good man to help her. In the car, she asked Steve, "Was it the SAS you were in?"

"No, Parachute Regiment, did nine years."

"Was it a good life in the army?" asked Cath.

"It was alright at first, but it's a young man's game and although part of me wishes I'd never left, I just knew that I needed to get out."

Cath wanted to ask more but she found herself falling asleep just as the dusk of the evening night came.

Chapter Nine

"What do you mean he's gone missing?" screamed Jake.

"I've told you, I set it up earlier and then not heard anything, but it's been all over the news. Don't take your tantrum out on me." replied Arthur.

"What if the police come looking for us, not only will I lose my job, but we could be in some serious shit."

"Don't be silly Jake, they're only junkies, who's gonna believe a word they say. Chances are that when the boy gets found, he'll end up in your care anyway."

Jake wasn't convinced. "I just don't like it; we have to be careful with what we do."

"Oh well it serves me right for doing something nice to surprise you. I'll remember that in future."

The arguing continued for the next hour. Then both parties sat quiet and watched the news together. The report was sketchy at best, as well as brief, but it did show a picture of Catherine Harrison, albeit not an up to date one. The report went on to mention that two people were in custody and were helping with enquires whilst a short statement was read by Patrick Fisher which asked for Catherine to come forward, or alternatively anyone who had seen her. Arthur turned to Jake, "there you see sweetie there's nothing that can tie it to us!"

"Okay, I'll check on the computer at work tomorrow to see if there's anything I can find out."

"You do that sausage, now come here." Then both men kissed on the sofa.

Patrick was done for the day. He was tired and drained and he was also tired of feeling tired and drained. In custody, Terry said little other than "no comment." Which wasn't helped by the fact he had a solicitor present during interview. Just the mere fact that Terry refused any comment when his own son was missing, signaled to the investigation team that there was more to this.

As for Sophie, on entering the custody suite and being examined by the medical team, she was sent straight to Hull Royal Infirmary. Although technically still in custody, she would not be fit for interview for at least a couple of days. Patrick didn't like it, but the fact was that Terry was going to have to be given bail, even though they had evidence of his possession of crack cocaine, it wasn't enough to keep him. However, they did seize his phone which would maybe turn up something. Even Patrick had to admit that in most cases, when a phone was seized, there usually was that much information on it that it was easy to convict. However, there hadn't been the time.

Patrick walked through his front door at about eleven o'clock and Molly, his wife, had already gone to bed. He took off his jacket and placed it on the back of the chair before heading straight to the drinks cabinet where he poured himself a large Jack Daniels before collapsing on the chair in front of the telly. Soon, he would be asleep.

Around the same time, Steve, Cath and the baby, were arriving at Wind Egg view in North Yorkshire – a sleepy little hatchet on the edge of Catterick Garrison. First, Steve had driven to the biker estate in Newcastle where he had seen his brother in arms briefly before getting the key to the cottage. He then made his way back down the A1. Making his way into the village, it seemed a world away from the hustle and bustle from the city – there was not even any street lighting, in fact even the main road was little more than a dirt track. Steve turned right off the road and into what appeared to be a cul-de-sac, which had a phone box on the edge, still with no street lighting. There were eight houses together in the shape of a horseshoe, most were holiday cottages with the odd one or two that were retirement homes. Steve continued along the road that was a mixture of shingle and mud and pulled up alongside the back door of the cottage. It was dark and due to the lack of light pollution from the big city, the stars seemed to shine brighter. Cath picked up the baby and made her way to the backdoor with Steve as the security light came on. Once inside, the smell was a mixture of coal fires and damp – it was obvious the place had not been used in a few months at least, however, the kitchen was brand new. Cath felt tired and weary, just as the baby began to stir.

"Get yourself sat down in the living room and feed the baby – I'll get the fire going and then bring the stuff in from the car" Steve said. Despite the fact Cath was irritable, she did as she was told. Steve lit the fire and brought in the shopping he'd bought from the Asda in Gateshead. By the time he had finished unpacking, Cath had fallen asleep on the sofa with the baby boy cradled, asleep in her arms. Steve knew full well that he couldn't leave her and the baby alone whilst she was coming down, plus it was the perfect location to hide, only three people knew they were there. Since Cath had fallen asleep downstairs, Steve took it upon himself to go upstairs and make up the bedrooms. There was even an old-fashioned cot. Tiredness soon swept over him and so he returned to Cath and the baby and ushered them both upstairs to bed.

Cath turned to Steve, "Steve, don't leave me till I'm right" she begged. He placed a reassuring hand on her shoulder and promised her that he wasn't going to.

Chapter Ten

Over the next week, Catherine began her rattle which took her to new dimensions of hell, however she was determined as she owed it to that baby to make sure he would make it to a safe place. All she had to do now was make sure that her will was strong enough. She had cramps all over her body, like a sharp knife twisting inside her guts. Every now and again she felt extreme nausea causing her to be sick, but most of the time all she could bring up was bile. She tried to sleep but it would not come, the only thing that did come was the hellish extent of her symptoms of withdrawal. All Cath could hear was the drummer inside her head and to combat it, she tried rocking herself. She felt cold, ice cold, however she perspired like she had a swamp fever. Every couple of hours, Steve checked in on her and brought her food and something to drink and even though she tried a few bites, she could not face the food. As slowly as time went, Cath's will got stronger, and she was determined to never find herself in this awful place again. Every now and again, Steve would sit beside her as he slung his arm around her, giving what comfort he could as she rocked – physically, it meant nothing, but emotionally, it was everything. The comfort to her pain that she needed.

The second day carried on much the same, but by the third and fourth, Cath began to feel the effects wearing – even managing to eat something and keep it down. It was almost as if she believed in herself that she was going to get through it. She was still irritable and at the same time exhausted. She began to think about everything she had done throughout her addiction which emotionally, was an extremely low point – the feelings of depression and guilt claimed her as a result of the things she had done to feed her habit, the people she had ripped off, the money she stole from family and the pain she had caused the people she loved most to go through. She prayed that God would forgive her, because she knew some of the people she'd ripped off, would never.

By the fifth and sixth day, she'd managed to find some sleep, granted it was light sleep at first, but at least it was sleep. Physically and emotionally, she was drained but she was pushing through.

By the seventh day, she began to think there was a light at the end of the tunnel. There was almost an elated feeling that she had done it, rising inside her.

During the week of Catherine's detox, Jake had been frantically checking the systems at work as well as monitoring the news. It was apparent that Patrick Fisher was in charge of the investigation. Jake toyed with the idea of ringing his office, but every time he picked up the phone, he soon put the receiver down again. In the end, Jake's curiosity got the better of him and he made the call.

Patrick was sat in his office at Clough Road Police Station, he was checking the details on Terry's phone, cross referencing telephone numbers – most were known drug dealers in the city. However, there was one number that was unaccounted for, could this be the missing link to finding the baby. Just then, his office phone rang.

"Patrick Fisher CID"

"Jake Sylvester here, Head of Child Services at East Riding Council."

Patrick listened, unsure what this phone call was about.

"Just a quick call to see if there has been any development in the missing child's case."

"I'm not in a position to comment on it at the moment as it is still under police investigation. May I ask why this is of any concern to you?"

Jake was on the backfoot and replied, "just like everyone else Mr Fisher, concerns for the infant and just to let you know that I have a suitable foster family if the boy is found safe and well."

Patrick was bemused by what he was hearing. "Firstly, Mr Sylvester, next of kin will be notified first regarding custody"

Jake stopped him there "oh I know that I'm just saying that we have a suitable foster family."

Patrick was annoyed. "Once this investigation is complete, should we need to contact you, we will go through the relevant channels." The officer's patience wore thin, and he placed the receiver down. Just at that moment, there was a knock at his door as a female inspector walked in. "Yes Eve, what is it?" demanded Patrick.

"Bad phone call gov?" replied the inspector.

Patrick sighed and replied, "just some idiot at the council, he said he was head of child services and that he had a foster family for our child. Why would he contact me directly? Bloody idiot. Anyways what have you got?"

"We have the CCTV back from Paragon station. Catherine Harrison boarded a train and got off at Leeds. The CCTV at Leeds station sees her getting into a car registered to a Steve Robinson. From what we can gather, Robinson used to be a Minder for Catherine's escorting agency."

"Good work inspector, anymore?"

"Yeah, I have an address for him in Leeds, but uniform have been and got no answer."

"Okay, I'm gonna put in a request for an arrest warrant for Robinson. What else do we know about him?"

"He served nine years in the Para's Gov."

Patrick looked at the inspector, "Well at least she's not taken the baby to some junkie scumbag. Send that request for the warrant through to the magistrates. Well done."

Chapter Eleven

It was going to be a lovely day in Wind Egg View as the dawn broke. Catherine, feeling more alive had woken early and was nursing a coffee when Steve entered the room. "How you feeling now Cath?" He asked, with genuine concern.

"More alive than what I have done for years, to be honest Steve. However, I don't know what I'm going to do with the baby."

Steve thought for a second and replied "we're going to have to do something with him soon Cath, because, not only does he need a birth certificate, he also needs to get checked over to make sure he's healthy.

Not to mention the vaccinations and inoculations the little man's gonna need."

Steve looked at Cath. "You do realise you can't keep him, you know that?"

"Yeah I know, I just want to give him a head start."

Steve replied, "the other thing is Cath, we can't stay here much longer, the police and public will be looking for us already."

Arthur wasn't happy with the situation. If it was found out about him and Jake there would be real prison time involved. He also knew that if Terry was in custody, it wouldn't take him long to squeal. Arthur knew that Terry would sell his own soul if it meant saving himself. All Arthur could think of was for Terry to be silenced forever. For the time being, Arthur would not say anything to Jake. However, his plan could potentially involve a murder charge if not done right. Arthur picked up the phone to ring a Lithuanian.

Chapter Twelve

North East Lincolnshire had the most fertile farming ground in the country. When Poland and Lithuania joined the EU, it was only a matter of time for those from the Eastern block hoping for a better life, travel to the UK. Along with this came organised crime. People were smuggled through the docks of Hull and Felixstow and sent to work on the farms, mainly men of working age. There were also some women, most were trafficked off to work as sex slaves. Verchenko was a villain of the highest order from the Eastern European block, starting his life as a conscript in the Lithuanian military, he was well adverse into using violence to get what he wanted. Even his second in command would fear him. Verchenko had no qualms about disposing of anybody that either crossed him or cost him money. There were rumours that he once was part of Russian Special Forces Spetsnaz. Now his main role, was one of gangmaster. Not only did he now have to keep an eye on the money which was sent home to his paymasters, but also he had to keep the workers in line. On one occasion he even broke the arm of a disgruntled employee only to force him back to work the next day with non-medical treatment. This was a clear message to the other workers. Verchenko was not to be crossed.

Arthur rang Verchenko "I have a job for you."

"Not over the phone" Verchenko hissed. "Meet me at the Humber Bridge Carpark tonight, 10pm." The phone line went dead.

Patrick Fisher returned to the office. The child kidnapping case was going nowhere. Officers from Leeds had been to Steven Robinson's apartment several times but no-one seemed to know where he was. It was known that he had picked up Cath and the last of the CCTV from the motorway cameras said his last destination was Newcastle. There was not enough for a search warrant. Hopefully today, information would come back from Terry's phone. This would give more information as to what had happened in the house on The Avenues. As for Terry's partner Sophie, by now, she had been discharged from Hull Royal Infirmary but said nothing on interview.

Just then, there was a knock on Patrick's office door. Eve stood there. "Gov, we've got the information from Terry's phone."

"Anything significant Eve?" Patrick asked.

"Just like we thought Gov, mainly dealer's numbers." However, there's another number we're not sure about."

"Go on." Patrick demanded.

"It's a cell phone in the Beverley area and it's registered to someone called Arthur White."

Patrick replied, "have you put Arthur White through the police computer?"

"No-one on the system called Arthur White has a criminal record Gov.

However, there are three Arthur Whites' living in Beverley."

"Well done Eve," said Patrick. "Get the Arthur Whites' addresses and go and interview them. Check the council tax records for the address."

"Yes Gov."

Chapter Thirteen

Humber Bridge carpark was almost empty. There looked to be two boy racers parked next to each other. On the other side of the carpark looked to be a courting couple, in a Ford Fiesta. As Arthur made his way around the carpark looking to see where Verchenko would be parked, just then to his right, he saw flashing lights from a black BMW. Arthur pulled up alongside, turned off his engine and climbed inside Verchenko's car. Verchenko was smoking and the smell was pungent from the stale nicotine. It was Verchenko who spoke first. "So what you want? Another boy to play with?"

Arthur felt intimidated by Verchenko. Although they'd only done business now and again, Arthur felt he knew what type of man Verchenko was. Arthur took a deep breath and said "I need you to kill somebody."

Verchenko smiled. "What the Fuck." He replied. "Who do you want me to fucking kill?"

"Nobody of any significance" Arthur replied. "Just a druggie. But I need you to make it look like an accident. Like he's overdosed himself."

Verchenko looked deep at Arthur. "Well that's the real trick isn't it, and its gonna cost you more."

Arthur swallowed, looking at the menace in Verchenko's eyes. "Ok, how much do you need?"

Verchenko replied, "I don't need fucking anything. I get what I fucking want."

"OK so how much?"

"Four thousand."

"OK that's fine. How soon can you do it?"

"Depends," replied Verchenko, "what's this fucking druggie done anyway?"

Arthur went on to explain the circumstances as to why Terry must be silenced.

Verchenko opened his glove box and pulled out a scrap of paper. He wrote down his bank details and handed the note over.

"In this bank account by weekend. Also, I need a description and an address for this fucking junkie. Once I'm paid, will take me a couple of days. Now fuck off you homosexual freak."

Arthur couldn't wait to get out of the car, it was almost a pleasure.

Before he'd climbed back into his own vehicle. Verchenko had already sped off towards the Humber Bridge. He looked around. Both the boy racers and the doggers were still in the same place. Arthur was pretty sure they would not have noticed him and made his way back home.

Chapter Fourteen

It was an early start for Patrick and Eve. They had tracked down all three Arthur Whites' in Beverley through the council records. The first Arthur White was a non-entity, he was staying in a care home with vascular dementia and according to his carers' did not even have access to a mobile phone.

Patrick and Eve had more luck with the second Arthur White. However, he was a truck driver nearing retirement and had spent the last month in Benidorm with his wife. This did not rule him out of the enquire but clearly, this Arthur White was not a suspect.

The last address was in Morton Lane in Beverley. It was Patrick who rang the doorbell just as Jake Sylvester was getting ready for work. Jake answered the door and recognised Patrick from the TV straight away. "Hello inspector, I take it that this is about the boy?" As soon as Jake said this he regretted it, just from the look in Patrick's eye.

"I'm sorry. We've not been introduced. I'm DCI Patrick Fisher from Humberside Police and this is my associate,lo Inspector Eve Lindstrom." At the same time Patrick and Eve clocked each other knowing something was amiss. "May I have your name sir?"

"Jake Sylvester, head of services at East Riding Child Services"

"Are you here alone?" Patrick asked.

"My husband Arthur is out. Is to do with the baby boy that has gone missing?" Jake asked again.

"I'm afraid I can't comment on that. These are just routine enquiries and I'm afraid I can't comment further. We would like to speak to Arthur however, I don't suppose you have his mobile number?"

Jake was on the spot, and Patrick knew it. As casually as Jake could fake a smile, he wrote down Arthurs number and handed it to the DCI. Jake smiled, "Are you sure you cannot tell me what this is about?"

Patrick replied. "Just routine enquiries, nothing to worry about. We won't waste any more of your time today sir."

Jake's fake smile was wearing thin as he closed the door. As Patrick walked away, the cogs in his mind were turning. Ultimately, it was almost as if the pieces were beginning to fit.

Patrick and Eve got into their unmarked Audi. Patrick then turned to Eve and said, "get me the number for Arthur White that was on Terry's phone." Then Patrick added, "cross reference it to this number."

Eve said, "it's a match Gov, what shall we do?"

Patrick swore lightly under his breath. "Fuck me" he said, and then he added "get a search warrant, that's what we're gonna do Eve. But right now I want to get back to the office."

Chapter Fifteen

Verchenko had found Terry. First he went to the bail hostel. Terry was a weasel of a man, looking older than his years and Verchenko could see this in his prey. Discreetly, during the day, Verchenko stalked Terry. On leaving the bail hostel in the morning, Terry and two accomplices had gone shoplifting in Hull City Centre. From here, Verchenko saw Terry on a pushbike on Spring Bank. From what he saw, was entering what looked like a crack house.

Two hours later Terry emerged, Verchenko's cover was never going to be blown. He was a seasoned operator. Whereas Terry was a seasoned junkie, totally unaware of his surroundings and the danger he was in. For the second time that day, Verchenko followed Terry into Hull City Centre. This time, Terry stopped outside a cash converters. Terry came out ten minutes later. Verchenko saw his chance. Approaching Terry he said "are you in the market for some gear?" Terry looked up at this mountain of a man. "What gear is it? Is it brown or white?"

"It's real good gear" Verchenko replied. Then he added "I'll do you a deal at 20, if you like it you can maybe sell for me." As Terry was oblivious to everything but his own addiction, he did not even consider that he did not know this man. Verchenko asked Terry "do you have somewhere we can go so you can test it?"

"There's a carpark around the corner"

"Show me the way." Verchenko said. "I have some cooking gear."

Verchenko and Terry were on the third floor of the King Billy carpark. Both looked around to see if there were any witnesses. Not that Terry was bothered, but Verchenko certainly was. "Where's the gear?" Terry asked. Verchenko put his hand in his pocket and pulled out a ball of substance. Known on the circuit as an 8 ball, it was a mixture of crack cocaine and pure heroin.

Terry's eyes widened when he saw what Verchenko was offering. Terry tried to make small talk to appease his supplier. Verchenko handed Terry a pipe as well as a lighter. "Cook it up my friend and you can sell it for me." Placing the pipe in his mouth, Terry inhaled. His eyes rolled into the back of his head. He tried to take a step backwards and fell on the hard floor. Terry's body began to spasm as white froth came out of his mouth. Soon, Terry's ears and nose were bleeding. Verchenko stood over him almost laughing as Terry's heart began to give way.

Verchenko knelt over his victim, there was no pulse in the side of Terry's neck. If he wasn't dead now, he would be in five minutes. Just another junkie in just another carpark. Verchenko's last job was to take the last of Terry's money. For one last time he looked around the carpark, but there was no-body. His job was complete.

Chapter Sixteen

In the interview room Sophie felt the worst she'd ever felt in her life, she was coming down from Crack, also as a new mother she had no idea where her child was. This was more painful than the withdrawals. She looked across at her solicitor and envied her lifestyle. Manicured nails, holding a briefcase, smart black shoes, immaculately turned out in a Nadine Merabi power suit. Sophie wondered to herself how the lawyer opposite had got everything right in her life whilst Sophie had got everything so wrong. When the solicitor spoke, it was tinged with empathy for Sophie's situation.

"Sophie, she said. I'm here to help you, but you've got to let me. You've got to start telling the investigating team what's happened. Also, you have to be honest about what's happened with the baby."

"You mean grass?" Sophie replied.

"Sophie, your baby could be in real danger. If something happens that you could have prevented, you could end up in jail for a long time."

Sophie looked across at her mentor. It was obvious she was speaking the truth.

The lawyer then added, "tell you what we can do, you can tell me everything and I'll prepare a statement. That way, you do not have to go and interview."

Sophie realised the gravity of her situation. She was looking at real time. "OK" Sophie replied, "I'll tell you what happened."

Catherine had made her way to the payphone at the end of the lane on Wind Egg View, she'd given it some thought, and it wasn't fair on the baby boy to keep him with her any longer. She rang Humberside Police and was eventually put through to Clough Road Police Station.

Patrick was sat in his office arranging a search warrant when he took the call.

"Patrick Fisher CID."

"It's Catherine Harrison."

"Where are you Catherine?" Patrick asked, with genuine concern.

"Don't worry about that, but I want to turn myself in." Catherine replied.

As Catherine spoke, it reassured Patrick that he was right on the money that Catherine would not harm a child.

Catherine continued, "the baby's OK, but he was in danger which is why I took him."

"That's OK Cath, we thought as much. But I need to know where you are so that this doesn't escalate any further."

"I'm up near Scotland" Catherine lied. "But I'm coming back soon. I had to take him Patrick. Terry was going to sell the baby to a nonce."

Again, as Catherine spoke, a light switched on in Patrick's mind. Everything was starting to add up. Just as Patrick pushed once more to find out where Catherine was, the line went dead.

The DCI replaced the receiver and almost immediately picked up the phone. "I want a trace on the last call that was into my office and I want it now." He did not wait for a response before he shouted in the office "LINDSTROM! WHERE THE FUCK IS MY SEARCH WARRANT?!"

Chapter Seventeen

Jake was mad, he'd been ringing Arthur all day with no answer. On top of this, Arthur had taken £4000 out of their joint account. Money which was supposed to be for their anniversary in Goa. Eventually, Arthur picked up. "What's going on Arthur? I've been ringing all day and worried sick! It's not like I've just met you, you know."

"I'm sorry love" Arthur replied. "I've been covering our tracks so we don't get caught."

"What's that supposed to mean? For god's sake, you know I look after you. By the way, the police were round earlier asking after you."

"Oh for god's sake!" Arthur replied. "This is never going to end!" Arthur went on to explain to Jake about the contract he instructed Verchenko to carry out on Terry.

As Jake listened, he could hear the concern in Arthur's voice. "So I take it that's where the £4000 has gone for our anniversary!"

"OMG, all you think about is money! If it keeps us in the clear, then it's money well spent."

Jake got angry, "Listen to me! It's not just Terry we have to worry about, but also that junkie bitch that took him! Get onto the phone to Verchenko again. Tell him to find Catherine Harrison and do the same to her!"

Arthur was crying now.

"It's no good crying Arthur!" Jake shouted. "Get Verchenko to kill that fucking bitch! Use the money out our joint account"

Arthur had calmed down. "OK, you're right."

"I know I'm right!" replied Jake. "I can be a real serious bitch when I wanna be!"

Chapter Eighteen

The baby boy was quiet as Catherine and Steve made their way back towards Yorkshire. Steve was cautious not to use the main roads, such as the A1, driving away from Catterick towards Leeds. Steve tried to remember the way using the B roads, from memory. The mood was quiet and it was Steve who broke the silence, "what you thinking?" he asked.

"Just wondering how we're going to hand the baby over."

"Just take it to the local nick," Steve replied. "Either way, we're both gonna get arrested."

Catherine realised Steve was right. At one time, Catherine called the shots when Steve worked for her. Now the roles were reversed and Catherine realised she had to listen to Steve. Ultimately, Steve should have had no loyalty to Catherine whatsoever. But the fact is, he came through when there was no-one else. Again there was a silence. Then Catherine looked at Steve and said "Thankyou." She added, "thankyou for all your help Steve. I wouldn't have come this far if it wasn't for you." Steve looked back and smiled. "No problem, I quite enjoyed it." He replied. "To be honest its been a lot better than my average day." He added, "I was getting a bit sick of watching daytime TV with Phillip bloody Schofield."

Back at Clough Road police station, the prepared statement that Sophie had given was the caveat which was needed to get both the search warrant and the arrest warrant on Arthur White and Jake Sylvester. As for Sophie, Patrick Fisher saw no reason to keep her so he arranged for bail. He was just about to send officers to pick up Terry when the call came through to the office that the body of Terry had been found in King Billy carpark. First indications were of an overdose. However, given the timing of Terry's demurs, Patrick asked for CCTV in the area. The fact was, the case had taken so many twists and turns but ultimately, there was a child still missing. Also, Patrick was aware that Catherine would have to hand the child over soon if she was to come off lightly.

As the same time that the warrant was executed for the search of Jake Sylvester's home, the man himself was at a meeting at the East Riding Council. The shocks and gasps from Jake's colleagues was evident as he was led out of the office in handcuffs and placed in the back of the meat wagon.

Police professionals meticulously searched the house of Jake and Arthur. It wasn't long before they found what they were looking for. Sickening images on a laptop. Also, a number of DVD's, all would have to be checked. The raid was well underway as Arthur White approached Morton Lane. Seeing the activity emerge at the house he shared with Jake. Arthur quickly bent down to pretend to tie his shoelace. Then he turned up the collar on his Boss jacket. As he stood up he quickly made a U-turn praying he would not be seen. Arthur had already made the call to Verchenko and deposited the cash. But right now, his priority was getting out of the area.

Chapter Nineteen

Being high up in the criminal fraternity, Verchenko had contacts in the Humberside Police. Officers were either on the payroll or they were blackmailed. He rang his informant from within CID. PC Sharon Taylor loved her job and role in the police force, but felt sickened every time Verchenko contacted her. He had been blackmailing her for the last three years. As a fresh recruit she engaged in a threesome with two men on New Years Eve and Verchenko had the film. On top of this, there was evidence on the film of her taking cocaine. It was more than enough for Verchenko to use leverage to get information. "Go on the police computer" he told her, "and get me the mobile phone number for Catherine Harrison."

Taylor did as she was told. After she handed over Catherine Harrison's number, she was about to add that these demands should stop. Verchenko had hung up before she had even finished her sentence.

Verchenko returned to his BMW and began to send a text. It read "Catherine this is DCI Patrick Fisher here, there's more to this case than we realise. I need you to meet me with the baby at the old abandoned steelworks in Scunthorpe at 11pm. I guarantee you will not be prosecuted, but this goes higher up than the investigation first thought and I need to protect Sophie's child. Lastly, do not contact the office, text me on this number only." Verchenko's trap was set.

Patrick Fisher was scrolling through the CCTV of Terry's last movements. Patrick knew it was not good when it became apparent that Terry's death was suspicious when CCTV saw Verchenko approach Terry. Then it followed them to the carpark. Within ten minutes, Verchenko leaves the carpark, alone. It was within the next hour that Terry's body was found.

"OK, does anybody know who this guy is?"

The office was silent, like a classroom on the first day of school. Eventually the CCTV followed Verchenko back to his car. As it drove away there was only two digits of his registration that could be picked up by the camera.

"OK guys and girls. Find out who that man is and bring him to me!" Patrick barked.

Within seconds, the CID office jumped into life.

Chapter Twenty

Arthur White knew where this was going. He knew he was looking at a life sentence, and he did not like it. Right up until this point his life had been carefree and empowering, until he had been with Jake. Arthur knew the police raid would find all the evidence that himself and Jake were sexual offenders and he was only too well aware of what happened to sexual offenders in prison. It might not be so bad if he was locked up with Jake for the rest of his life, at least they would have each other. And again, Arthur re-evaluated his options and he knew this would never be the case. He felt that what he had with Jake Sylvester was so special, it justified killing Terry. But in the cold light of day he realised his justifications were wrong. The fact was, he and Jake were predatory pedophiles that had paid to have a man killed to cover their tracks. Arthur knew his life was never gonna be the same again.

He found himself outside of the Hull Minster, in Hull's Market Place. As he walked inside, he felt the coldness of the interior. He picked up a bible from the pew, looked up to the altar and offered himself a little prayer. No God came and put a reassuring hand on his shoulder. This was it, there was no other way out. He left the seat and made his way towards the back where the stairs would take him upto the roof. With each step, Arthur cried more tears. He reached the top of Hull Minster and looked out at the skyline. Just at that moment his phone rang. Arthur did not recognise the number and just threw it on the floor. "This is it," he said to himself. Then Arthur White threw himself off the ledge and fell to his death.

Chapter Twenty One

Steve was filling up his car with petrol whilst Catherine changed the baby in Costa Coffee. Catherine checked her mobile phone. She'd made a point of keeping it turned off whilst she detoxed. She read the message from Patrick Fisher. Even though it was strange, she did not dismiss it. After she finished changing the baby, she came out to Steve and showed him the text.

"OK," Steve replied," if that's what he wants, we're in Bradford now. Scunthorpe is only three hours away." Steve put his car into 1st and made his way to the M180.

The CID room was alive with activity. The news came through that within the hour Arthur white had committed suicide at the Hull Minster. He had left no note but when uniform went to the top of the Minster, they found Arthur Whites mobile phone. Immediately Patrick put a request in to forensics. The details in Arthur Whites phone needed to be checked into as top priority. Patrick knew it was a given that there would probably be indecent images on it, but it was the other information that Patrick wanted. Were there any messages between Arthur White and Terry? Also, was there a link between White and the mysterious man with Terry when he died? Patrick's instincts told him that there were.

At the same time as forensics were going through the mobile phone, information was coming in on the mysterious assassin. A full registration was picked up by the Humber Bridge cameras. It wasn't long before they had identified Verchenko. The information they had was sketchy. But it linked Verhenko to a mobile phone. Within an hour local officers were dispatched to arrest and detain Verchenko. In the meantime, it was just a case of waiting. The waiting was the hardest part. It was intense. Almost like pre-nerves before a cup final. Patrick knew it was going to be a long night. And he called his wife to say as much. The response was typical as she hung up on him.

Chapter Twenty Two

Steve, Catherine and the baby approached the outskirts of Scunthorpe. Initially, Steve wanted to do a reconnaissance on the site where they were supposed to meet Patrick Fisher at the steel works. Steve had done many missions with the Parachute Regiment where the reconnaissance was key for a successful outcome. However, they were still early and the Autumn sun had not yet set. By about 8pm, Steve drove past the site. There was no security on the gate. As Steve approached, he looked at the flimsy lock holding the ineffective chain together. He returned his Suzuki, opened the boot and retrieved a screwdriver. He returned to the gate, shoved the screwdriver through the lock and with three turns the lock broke free. However, Steve was not going to enter the site at this stage. He looked around at the baron industrial estate and the only noise seemed to be coming from the factory nextdoor. He returned to Cath and the baby. "We'll park around the corner," he said. "Grab a coffee and we'll just wait it out."

Patrick Fisher and the team at CID thought they'd struck gold. Not only had they gained access to Verchenko's phone but it was also apparent that Arthur White had rang him. There was a clear digital link between the two. They also downloaded the messages that Verchenko had sent, it soon became apparent how much of a bad man Verchenko was, how high up in the criminal food chain he was. Then the sinister message Verchenko had sent to Catherine Harrison came up on the system. It soon became apparent to Patrick that Verchenko was planning to kill Catherine. Patrick grabbed his coat and made for the door. As he was leaving, instructed Eve to contact Lincolnshire Police. Verchenko was to be arrested on suspicion of murder. Time was ticking now, it was almost 10.30pm.

Steve and Catherine, with their precious cargo, made their way back to the steelworks. On arrival, the gates were open. Something didn't sit right with Steve. The more he thought about it, the more suspicious Steve became. "Why would Patrick Fisher choose to meet here and not at a hospital and not a police station? This doesn't feel right Cath, you know."

"You're telling me!" Cath replied. "Have you got a weapon?"

Steve made light of the question. "Just the fists that the Parachute Regiment gave me."

As they drove into the compound, the road twisted to the right. Next to a container bar, a dark car flashed it's lights. Slowly, Steve drove up to the BMW. In the dark it was hard to tell who was inside. Steve's instinct told him to get ready. As the window in the BMW came down, Steve saw the barrel of a revolver. Within a second, Steve put his Suzuki into reverse and aggressively pressed the accelerator. At that point, two shots were fired. One hit in the front windscreen of Steve's car, but not smashing it. Steve put his car into 1st and slammed on the accelerator aiming for the BMW's side door. Verchenko saw what was happening and undid his seatbelt. As the two vehicles connected, the airbag in Verchenko's car exploded. Verchenko was dazed but not out of the game. Steve jumped out of his car and made for the BMW. As he climbed out of the passenger seat, Verchenko took aim. But Steve was too fast. With all the strength of a rugby tackle, Steve slammed the passenger door on Verchenko's arm, and again another crack as the revolver ejected another round. The pistol fell out of Verchenko's hand into the night. Steve Robinson however, was not finished. Steve grabbed Verchenko's wounded arm. Verchenko screamed in pain as Steve yanked his body towards the sill of the car door, Steve then began to brutally slam the door several times on Verchenko's head. Verchenko was down but not out. Pulling a knife from his jacket, he thrust the blade into Steve's upper leg. Steve felt the pain but the adrenaline was running. Over Steve's shoulder to the left was a sudden crack of a pistol and a bullet flew past Steve's ear like a flying hornet. The bullet hit Verchenko straight between the eyes, Verchenko did not move, he was done. Steve turned round to see Catherine stood behind him holding Verchenko's smoking pistol.

In the distance, the sirens of police cars were approaching. Steve looked at Catherine, as she held the revolver. "Well done girl." He complimented her. The look in her eye said that Catherine had no regrets. At that point, several police cars approached. Leading the way, Patrick Fisher got out of the vehicle.

Chapter Twenty Three

The activity around the steelworks was going to continue for some time. Patrick was pleased with his work. Ultimately, Sophie's baby was safe and now being checked over at Hull Royal Infirmary. Catherine Harrison and Steve Robinson were both arrested at the scene and taken into police custody. Ultimately, Patrick would go out of his way to make sure there were very few charges. Catherine had taken the baby to protect it and ultimately Sophie had given her permission. Robinson however, could be done for aiding and abetting but given the nights' events, The Crown Prosecution Service were unlikely to charge.

As for Jake Sylvester, he had been placed on remand and was looking at a lengthy sentence and given his position within the council and his offences, the case could even be heard in The Old Bailey.

The media were everywhere of course, talking up the story and trying to get an interview with Patrick. Patrick looked at Eve. "You do the media interview on this one Inspector. I'm going home for arguments with the wife." He smiled and added, "well done!"

Chapter Twenty Four

John Smith received a letter from his wife whilst on D Wing in HMP Hull, she had forgiven him for his drinking if he promised to stop, and with that they could resume their marriage together. It was the calling Smith needed. The last time he went to the pub, he started a fight with a Sunday league football player and when the police turned up he assaulted an officer, hence the reason he was in prison.

This was his last day before freedom beckoned. On leaving his cell, he looked across the wing and saw the face of a man who had caused him so much pain. It was Jake Sylvester. Under his breath, Smith whispered to himself "thankyou God."

Smith's cellmate at the time was a lifer called Christopher Chinwell, but he was known as Chinny. Three murders under his belt for a botched armed robbery. Chinny was never getting out. Whilst Smith and Chinny shared a cell, Smith helped him read the letters he received from his family and helped him write the letters back home. Just as he was packing his gear, Smith pointed Sylvester out to Chinny. "See that bastard there? He's been interfering with my babies. Do us a favour, take care of him."

Four hours later, Jake Sylvester was found dead in the shower block. No-one seemed to know what had happened to him. But his throat had been slit open and he had been castrated. The scene was horrific and Jake Sylvester would have died in a great deal of pain. No-one was ever charged.

Printed in Great Britain
by Amazon